STO

PARKER PIG, ESQUIRE

PARKER PIG, ESQUIRE

Story and pictures by
TOMIE DE PAOLA

Hawthorn Books, Inc. Publishers New York

FOR
Philip, who is Parker,
Mia, Moya and Brian.

Parker Pig, Esquire, had a nice old house called the Folly in the little town of Settle in Yorkshire.

One day he decided to invite some of his London friends for a holiday.

He sat right down and wrote them a letter. They answered by return mail and said they would be there late Friday afternoon, and could they bring a visitor from America?

Parker called and said, "Of course, a visitor from America would be very welcome."

"There he is!" said Mia. "Goodness, look at that hat."

"He looks well," said Brian. "His shoes are muddy as usual."

"I wonder if his house is still messy," said Moya.

"Boy, I'm looking forward to this holiday," said Tom. "Wait'll I write my friends back home in America."

"Hello," said Parker. "Get in the car. We'll go to the Folly immediately!"

They arrived at the Folly in a few minutes. It was a nice, big old house. Inside, the sitting room was warm and cozy with a big fire burning in the fireplace. It wasn't very neat though. It wasn't exactly dirty either, just a little messy.

"I knew it," said Mia.

"Could have guessed," said Brian.

"Untidy," said Moya.

"I think it's great. Real lived in," said Tom.

"Come in. I'll make a nice hot cup of tea," said Parker.

That night after a simple but good supper on dishes that didn't quite match and a wrinkled tablecloth, Parker said, "Well, how do you think everything looks?"

"I'm glad you asked," said Mia. "Don't you ever dust? All those papers and magazines. Really, Parker."

"You're always so wrinkled, Parker," said Brian. "Why don't you pull yourself together?"

"You should really arrange this room better," said Moya. "Such a hodgepodge."

"I'm having a great time," said Tom.

"Oh dear," said Parker, suddenly looking at the room and himself. "It is a bit confused, isn't it? Well, I'll do something about it immediately—or tomorrow, anyway. But first, let's have a nice hot cup of tea before bedtime."

That night Parker couldn't sleep.
"They're right," he said. "This place is a mess and so am I. Always a little off. Wrinkled, lumpy. The sitting room is awful."

Parker got up out of bed and started in.
He shifted furniture around the living room
and stacked the papers and magazines neatly.
He pressed the tablecloth and napkins and
his clothes. He worked all night.

In the morning he brought hot tea to each of his guests in bed and said, "Hello, breakfast will be ready immediately."

All the guests got up and dressed and went down to the sitting room for breakfast.

The room was shining clean. Parker was in very neat clothes. He was even wearing a tie.

"My!" said Mia.

"Good show!" said Brian.

"Heavens!" said Moya.

"Wow!" said Tom.

As they ate breakfast Parker would jump up and brush every crumb of toast that fell on the table into a little silver scoop. He sat stiffly so as not to wrinkle his suit. Then he did the washing up right away instead of sitting and chatting over a second cup of coffee.

Later they went for a walk in the hills.
"Please take your muddy shoes off before
going into the house," said Parker.

They sat in front of the fire and Mia
started to curl up on the sofa. Parker jumped
up and put a cloth under her stocking feet.
  Brian put his cigarette out in the ash tray.
Parker rushed up and emptied it immediately.

Moya pulled a chair closer to the fire and when she got up from it, Parker moved it right back.

Tom said, "I'm going out for a walk." He wasn't having a very good time.

Things went on like this for two days. It was awful. Parker stood or sat around stiffly. The room was always spick-and-span—too spick-and-span. No one felt comfortable.

One night Parker said, "I must go to the launderette immediately to do some washing. I'll be back very soon."

As soon as he left, all his friends began talking at once.

"What's the matter with him?" said Mia.

"Very tense, very tense. I think he's going off his head," said Brian.

"Not much fun, is he? I feel like going home," said Moya.

"Boy, are you people dumb!" said Tom. "I liked this whole place and Parker better when he was all wrinkled and comfortable and relaxed! Why did you have to change him?"

At that all the friends looked at one another and realized that they *had* tried to change their friend Parker. What's more, they had succeeded and that's why they weren't having a good time.

Quickly they put the room back the way
it had been.

They got Parker's old wrinkled coat and
pants from his closet and when Parker came
in they said, "We're sorry, Parker, dear. We
like you better when you are yourself instead
of when you are trying to please us. Please put
your old clothes on. Let's have fun as we
did before."

Now the Folly and Parker were a little
untidy again. Everyone had a wonderful time.
And they all go to visit Parker Pig, Esquire, at
the Folly, Settle, Yorkshire, for every holiday
and they never try to change him anymore.